THE BEDTIME Book

TODD PARR

Megan Tingley Books

LITTLE, BROWN AND COMPANY

NEW YORK BOSTON

To Mr. Biggles Bear

Also by Todd Parr

A complete list of Todd's books and more information can be found at toddparr.com.

About This Book

The illustrations for this book were created on a drawing tablet using an iMac, starting with bold black lines and dropping in color with Adobe Photoshop. This book was edited by Megan Tingley and Esther Cajahuaringa and designed by Lynn El-Roeiy. The production was supervised by Kimberly Stella, and the production editor was Marisa Finkelstein. The text was set in Todd Parr's signature font.

But no one is ready for bed.

The puppy has to brush his teeth.

The narwhal needs to take her bath.

The raccoon has the hiccups.

HICCUP!

HICCUP!

HICCUP!

HICCUP!

The bear is hungry.

The baby goats are still jumping on the bed.

The lion needs to brush his mane.

And the kitties are ready for their bedtime story.

But the pig found a giant spider in her room.

The hippopotamus can't find his pajama bottoms.

The elephant heard a noise in the closet.

The beaver has a toothache.

The dog has to go potty.

The giraffe's bed is too small.

The skunk is thirsty.

And Mr. Biggles the Bear is missing!

But the sheep are still counting sheep.

A fly is keeping the cow awake.

The bear has a tummy ache.

The hamster can't stop running.

And the polar bears are chilly.

BRR!

The penguins need their night-light.

And the bunny wants one last hug and kiss.
Good night!

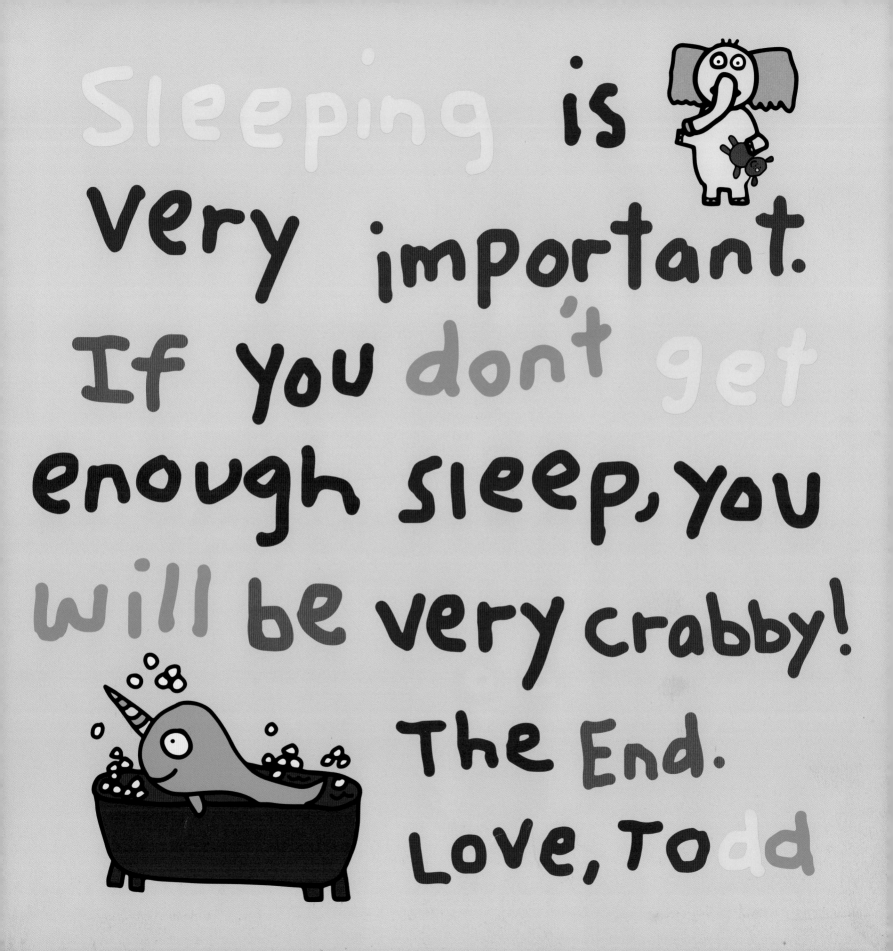

Sleeping is very important. If you don't get enough sleep, you will be very crabby! The End. Love, Todd